Elephant Sighs

by Ed Simpson

A SAMUEL FRENCH ACTING EDITION

New York Hollywood London Toronto
SAMUELFRENCH.COM

Copyright © 2009 by Ed Simpson

ALL RIGHTS RESERVED

CAUTION: Professionals and amateurs are hereby warned that *ELEPHANT SIGHS* is subject to a Licensing Fee. It is fully protected under the copyright laws of the United States of America, the British Commonwealth, including Canada, and all other countries of the Copyright Union. All rights, including professional, amateur, motion picture, recitation, lecturing, public reading, radio broadcasting, television and the rights of translation into foreign languages are strictly reserved. In its present form the play is dedicated to the reading public only.

The amateur and professional live stage performance rights to *ELEPHANT SIGHS* are controlled exclusively by Samuel French, Inc., and licensing arrangements and performance licenses must be secured well in advance of presentation. PLEASE NOTE that amateur Licensing Fees are set upon application in accordance with your producing circumstances. When applying for a licensing quotation and a performance license please give us the number of performances intended, dates of production, your seating capacity and admission fee. Licensing Fees are payable one week before the opening performance of the play to Samuel French, Inc., at 45 W. 25th Street, New York, NY 10010.

Licensing Fee of the required amount must be paid whether the play is presented for charity or gain and whether or not admission is charged.

Stock/professional licensing fees quoted upon application to Samuel French, Inc.

For all other rights than those stipulated above, apply to: Samuel French, Inc.

Particular emphasis is laid on the question of amateur or professional readings, permission and terms for which must be secured in writing from Samuel French, Inc.

Copying from this book in whole or in part is strictly forbidden by law, and the right of performance is not transferable.

Whenever the play is produced the following notice must appear on all programs, printing and advertising for the play: "Produced by special arrangement with Samuel French, Inc."

Due authorship credit must be given on all programs, printing and advertising for the play.

ISBN 978-0-573-69732-6   Printed in U.S.A.   #29175

No one shall commit or authorize any act or omission by which the copyright of, or the right to copyright, this play may be impaired.

No one shall make any changes in this play for the purpose of production.

Publication of this play does not imply availability for performance. Both amateurs and professionals considering a production are strongly advised in their own interests to apply to Samuel French, Inc., for written permission before starting rehearsals, advertising, or booking a theatre.

No part of this book may be reproduced, stored in a retrieval system, or transmitted in any form, by any means, now known or yet to be invented, including mechanical, electronic, photocopying, recording, videotaping, or otherwise, without the prior written permission of the publisher.

MUSIC USE NOTE

Licensees are solely responsible for obtaining formal written permission from copyright owners to use copyrighted music in the performance of this play and are strongly cautioned to do so. If no such permission is obtained by the licensee, then the licensee must use only original music that the licensee owns and controls. Licensees are solely responsible and liable for all music clearances and shall indemnify the copyright owners of the play and their licensing agent, Samuel French, Inc., against any costs, expenses, losses and liabilities arising from the use of music by licensees.

IMPORTANT BILLING AND CREDIT REQUIREMENTS

All producers of *ELEPHANT SIGHS* *must* give credit to the Author of the Play in all programs distributed in connection with performances of the Play, and in all instances in which the title of the Play appears for the purposes of advertising, publicizing or otherwise exploiting the Play and/or a production. The name of the Author *must* appear on a separate line on which no other name appears, immediately following the title and *must* appear in size of type not less than fifty percent of the size of the title type.

ELEPHANT SIGHS was first produced by Keystone Repertory Theater, Barbara Blackledge, Artistic Director, on June 17, 1998, under the direction of David Zarko, with setting by Brian Jones, lighting by Renee Cooper, costumes by Lindy Dipre, and stage management by Donald Robert Fox, with the following cast:

DINK FEENEY	David Tabish
JOEL BIXBY	Derek MacMahon
NICK WHALEN	Patrick Ferraro
PERRY LATIMER	Geoff Gould
LEO APPLEGATE	Ted Brunetti, Sr.

ELEPHANT SIGHS was subsequently produced by the Occasional Theater in association with Jeff Murray, Nicolette Chaffey, and Theatre/Theater at Theatre/Theater, Los Angeles on August 29, 1998, under the direction of Michael Lilly, with setting by Catherine Coke, lighting by C.C. Winston, costumes by Sandy Gayle, and stage management by Henry Lide, with the following cast:

DINK FEENEY	*Jack Kehler
JOEL BIXBY	Kirk Baily
NICK WHALEN	John Loprieno
PERRY LATIMER	David Wells
LEO APPLEGATE	Alan Bergmann

* Later Randy Ball

CHARACTERS

(In order of appearance)

JOEL BIXBY – 30s. A well-dressed, uptight, emotionally guarded lawyer. A newcomer and a fish out of water.

DINK FEENEY – 50s-60s. A kind, smallish, perpetually gleeful and delighted man devoted to his wife, family, and friends.

NICK WHALEN – 30s-40s. A volatile contractor beset by life. Passionate. Wears his heart on his sleeve.

PERRY LATIMER – 30s-40s. Nick's best friend and a former minister who now sells insurance. A decent man in the midst of a crisis of faith.

LEO APPLEGATE – 60s. Large, loquacious, sentimental, and the beloved leader of the group. A fast food connoisseur.

ACKNOWLEDGMENTS

I am particularly indebted to three wonderful directors, collaborators, and good friends who, at various times, helped bring "the Guys" to life: John Gulley, David Zarko, and Michael Lilly.

As always, I am grateful for the ususal band of friends and family, especially Dave Tabish (*the* "Dink"); Ken Scales; Brenda Lilly (thanks for my career!); Dave Wells (*always* there); Barbara Blackledge; Brian Jones; Geoff Gould; Richard Herd; Michael Mahoney; John Martello; Bill Shick; Randy Ball; Tom Parkhill; David Gigliotti; Rob Paty; Rob Gretta; The Noon Basketball Guys; Sally Piper; the faculty and students at Indiana University of Pennsylvania's Department of Theater; the Department of Theater at the University of North Carolina-Greensboro; my students and colleagues at High Point University; Alan Cook; Barry Bell; William Martin; Gentle Gennett; Jan Powell; the music of Randy Newman and Loudon Wainwright, III; with love to Martha Pearce, Becky Andrews, and the entire Simpson Clan (with a special thanks to Johnny Whalen); my great kids, Ben and Molly; and, finally, to my bride, Cyd, for answering my sighs.

– *Ed Simpson*
2009

Dedicated, in loving memory, to my Dad,

Harold E. Simpson
1913-1997

"What about it?!"

(*SETTING: A small meeting room in the process of being renovated.*)

(*AT RISE:* **JOEL** *enters the room, looking about tentatively. He wanders around the room for a moment. Uncomfortable, he turns to leave. Then…*)

DINK. Christ on a bike!

(*Startled,* **JOEL** *cries out.* **DINK** *sits up by the radiator where he has been lying, unseen, trying to adjust the heat.*)

Is it cold in here to you?

JOEL. (*trying to recover*) What?

DINK. I'm freezing, I'll tell you *that* right now. Listen. You hear that?

(*A mystified* **JOEL** *listens. A beat.*)

JOEL. No.

DINK. Me neither. Heat's off.

(*placing his hand on the radiator*)

Feel that.

(**JOEL** *tentatively places his hand on the radiator.*)

Huh?

JOEL. It's cold.

DINK. (*on his hands and knees and peering behind the radiator*) Betchyer ass it's cold. Heat's off. Lemme just…Ah! O.K. That's what I thought. That's what I thought. Where's the…damn.

JOEL. Uh…is there anything I can –

DINK. (*sitting up again and looking about the room.*) The *knob* is what it is. Looks kinda like a hockey puck. About so big.

JOEL. *(looking around the room)* I don't –
DINK. There it is. Gimme that, will you?

    *(**DINK** ducks his head behind the radiator again.)*

JOEL. *(looking around)* Where? I'm sorry –
DINK. *(Head still behind the radiator, he points.)* Under *that* over there. You see that thing?

    *(**JOEL** has finally spied the knob and crosses to retrieve it.)*

JOEL. Oh!
DINK. Gimme that, willya?
JOEL. *(gives the knob to **DINK**)* Here you are.
DINK. *(good-naturedly)* Keeps falling off, you know what I'm saying? It falls off, people kick it accidentally, kids come in here – they throw it around, think it's a Frisbee or something. Next thing you know, you go to turn on the heat and you can't find the knob.
JOEL. I see.

    *(**DINK** whangs on the knob with his wrench a couple of times.)*

DINK. There you go.

    (sitting up)

    That's got her. *Now* listen.

    (They both listen. A slight "hiss" can be heard.)

    You hear that?
JOEL. I hear that.
DINK. *Now* we'll get some heat in here. Huh?
JOEL. I should think.
DINK. Now we'll get some heat. Thanks…umm –
JOEL. Joel. Joel Bixby?
DINK. Howya doin'?

    *(Shakes **JOEL**'s hand.)*

    Dink Feeney.
JOEL. Dick –

DINK. Dink.

JOEL. Dink.

DINK. Real name's Donald but nobody but my mother and the cops call me that, you know what I'm sayin'? I been Dink ever since I was a little bastard.

(Hand on the radiator.)

Oh yeah. Oh yeah. Now it's comin. You feel that?

(JOEL puts his hand on the radiator.)

JOEL. Yes indeed. Toasty.

(pause)

Um…anyway. Leo Applegate asked me if I'd…you know. Drop by tonight.

DINK. Oh, hey – wait a minute. You're the guy.

JOEL. Beg pardon?

DINK. You're taking Walter's place.

JOEL. Well, you see –

DINK. Oh, Jesus Christ. That about ruined me. Honest to God – there's not been a day gone by the last year I don't think about Walt and that day. Holy Christ!

JOEL. Really?

DINK. Died right on top of me, for God's sake. You know that?

JOEL. *(taken aback)* No, I didn't. I mean, Leo told me your friend died but –

DINK. An experience I don't want to re-live, let me tell you. I'm standin right there next to him and he just toppled. Like a tree I'm talking. Right on top of me. Unbelievable. One second he's there, he's fine, we're shooting the breeze. Next thing I know – tim-ber! Broke my heart.

JOEL. Well –

DINK. You don't look like him, y'know.

JOEL. I…should I?

DINK. You're about his height, maybe a little taller but Walter was a big guy, let me tell you. Musta been 230-240. Big, big man. I mean, I should know, right? You ever had a 240 pound dead man lying on top of you?

JOEL. No.

DINK. Ain't for nothin it's called dead weight, let me tell you. Jesus. I still get choked up thinkin about it.

JOEL. I can imagine.

(a beat)

Anyway, I –

DINK. Excuse me, Joel, but you mind if I do a few things here while you talk? I mean, I'm listening – I just gotta get things set up before the rest of the guys get here. That O.K.?

JOEL. Oh sure. Sure. Do whatever.

DINK. *(pleasantly)* Thanks.

JOEL. So, anyway –

DINK. Get that end of the table, willya?

(They slide a table to one side.)

JOEL. – when Leo dropped by my office the other day –

DINK. Thanks.

*(**DINK** walks into the closet and **JOEL** follows to just outside the door.)*

JOEL. – and – you're welcome – and invited me to stop by tonight to participate in the activities –

DINK. *(from inside the closet)* Uh-huh.

JOEL. – I said "Certainly" despite the fact that, ordinarily, I'm not much of a joiner. I don't join clubs, I don't join groups – social or professional. I'm just not an organizational man.

*(**DINK** comes out carrying an American flag on a pole.)*

But...well, having just moved to town and setting up a new practice – personal injury and divorce primarily – I thought it would, you know, be an outstanding opportunity to interface with some people, make some business contacts –

(**DINK** *has set the flag down and snaps off a salute and crosses to folding chairs.*)

JOEL. *(cont.)* – but –

(**JOEL** *also snaps off a salute – surprising himself – and crosses to* **DINK**.)

– but – and…well, now, this is really rather embarassing –

DINK. *(Hands* **JOEL** *a couple of folding chairs.)* Here you go, Joel.

(**JOEL** *takes the chairs.*)

JOEL. It wasn't until after Leo had left my office that I realized I didn't actually know just *what* it was I'd agreed to participate *in*.

(*A beat as* **DINK** *continues to get chairs.*)

I mean, Leo is quite an impressive personality. He has the most amazing way of talking to you. Frankly, after a couple of minutes I would have agreed to anything. Very persuasive. Mesmerizing, actually. Quite remarkable.

DINK. *(pointing off to one side)* Put 'em over there.

(**JOEL** *unfolds the chair and puts it where* **DINK** *indicated.*)

JOEL. Anyway, he was rather vague about what goes on other than to say I'd meet some interesting people and that it wasn't illegal.

DINK. *(counting chairs)* 1, 2, 3 –

JOEL. I mean, it isn't is it? Illegal?

(*He laughs. A beat.*)

DINK. Two more.

(*Crossing to get more chairs.* **JOEL** *follows.*)

JOEL. Anyway, Leo suggested –

DINK. You're new in town, huh?

JOEL. Wha…uh – yes. We bought a place over on Poplar Street. Big back yard. Kids love it. Anyhow –

(getting a couple of chairs)

DINK. Hey – so you got kids, huh?

JOEL. Yes. A girl and a boy. 7…no – 8. 8 and 4. Anyway –

DINK. I got two grown daughters and a grandkid on the way. How about *that*?

JOEL. Well…how *about* that?

DINK. *(beaming with pride)* Thanks.

(taking chairs to join the others)

JOEL. You're welcome. Anyway, I –

DINK. So what line of business you in?

JOEL. I'm…I'm a lawyer. As I said, I've just opened a practice in town. In fact, just yesterday I got my first client. Personal injury suit.

DINK. Oh. Lawyer, huh?

JOEL. *(with a bit of an edge, waiting for the inevitable remark)* Yes. A lawyer.

DINK. Hey – that's O.K. by me, Joel. Nothin to be ashamed of.

JOEL. Thank you.

DINK. Fact of the matter is my daughter who's goin to have the kid? Married to a lawyer. Very successful, Joel. Makes a killin. They got this new house? Like a mansion. I mean, they got a hot tub big enough to choke a horse it's so big.

(a beat)

JOEL. Really?

DINK. Makes a hell of a lot of money. Most of it's legal, I think.

JOEL. I see. Anyway, as I said to Leo –

DINK. Yeah – when did you see Leo, anyway?

JOEL. The other day. He dropped by my office.

DINK. Tuesday?

JOEL. No – Thursday, I think.

DINK. Wasn't Tuesday though?

JOEL. No. Why?

DINK. Cause I saw him on Tuesday – hold that, will ya? – and he didn't look so good.

JOEL. He didn't?

DINK. He did not. Walter kickin the bucket hit Leo pretty hard. They'd been friends for years and years, were around the same age, had a lot in common. Used to go to Pirates games back when they were good. I think they even took some vacations together. You know.

JOEL. I see.

DINK. They were close. Very, very close. Truth be known? Leo loved Walter. I mean, with a *manly* kind of love, you know what I'm saying. Nothing...well nothing – you know.

JOEL. Right.

DINK. Although I knew a guy like that one time. In Louisville, Kentucky. As fine a fellow as you'd ever want to know.

(*A mystified beat. Then...*)

JOEL. Great.

DINK. I say just let people live their lives, Joel. Know what I'm saying?

JOEL. Yes.

DINK. So, anyhow, Leo's taking it pretty hard. Crap...we all are. But – what the hell? – life goes on, right? Walter would be the first to say that. That was the kinda guy he was.

(*From a box,* **DINK** *pulls out a red army "soft cap," festooned with various ribbons and medals and with "Walt" embroidered on its side.* **DINK** *puts the cap on* **JOEL**. *It is too large for* **JOEL**'s *head.*)

Here...this was Walt's. I think you should wear it.

(*Clapping* **JOEL** *on the back.*)

Good to have you on board, Joel.

JOEL. But I don't –

(**NICK WHALEN** and **PERRY LATIMER** *enter.* **NICK** *is carrying a tool box and has a couple of 2x4's under his arm. Under his overcoat,* **PERRY** *is wearing a jogging suit and carries a styrofoam coffee cup and a small stack of paperback books.*)

NICK. You flipped me the bird, Perry.

PERRY. No I didn't –

NICK. You flipped me the bird.

DINK. *(greeting them)* Hey, hey guys!

PERRY. You cut in front of my car, you almost ran me off the road, but I did not give you the finger.

NICK. You flipped me off!

PERRY. I didn't!

NICK. How could you do that? You're a minister, for Christ's sake. A man of God.

PERRY. Not anymore, Nick. Not anymore.

NICK. You are a holy man, Perry. How's that supposed to make me feel? It's like God himself giving you the finger. You really hurt me.

(hand to his heart)

Right here, man.

PERRY. Come on –

DINK. You gave Nick the finger, Perry?

PERRY. No! I just shook my fist at him.

NICK. Oh, great! What – that supposed to make me feel better? That's just as bad.

PERRY. No it isn't –

NICK. A man of the cloth shakes a fist at you? I mean, shit! I feel terribly unclean, Perry. You may have condemned me to hell there!

PERRY. Jeez.

NICK. *(to* **DINK***)* Christ – it's cold in here.

DINK. Give it a few minutes.

(hand on the radiator)

Feel that?

NICK. *(looking at the hole in the wall)* Damned place is falling apart. Lookit that. *(picks up a hammer)* They shoulda hired me to do this job, you know what I'm saying?

DINK. *(with a shrug)* What can you do?

NICK. You know why they didn't, don't you?

(He taps on the wall a couple of times with his hammer.)

DINK. Yeah, but – gee – you know, Nicky, maybe you shouldn't do that, you know?

NICK. Bastards. I mean, Dink, you seen my work.

DINK. Oh…well, yeah. Sure.

NICK. Nothing but quality, Dink. Craftmanship. Am I right?

(He bangs another hole in the wall. A beat.)

I'll get that later.

JOEL. Jeez.

PERRY. *(seeing JOEL)* Oh. Hi.

JOEL. Hello – Joel Bixby.

DINK. Oh yeah – Perry Latimer, Nick Whalen – this is… what is it again?

JOEL. Joel. Joel Bix –

DINK. *(to all)* Yeah, right – Joel. You'll like him, guys.

(then, with a laugh)

He's a great sport.

JOEL. *(totally mystified)* I am?

PERRY. That's…that's Walt's hat.

JOEL. Yes.

(A brief pause. Then…)

PERRY. *(pleasantly, shaking hands)* Nice to meet you, Joel.

JOEL. Reverend –

PERRY. Oh – no. No. Please. I mean, I'm not one any more.

JOEL. Oh. Right. Sorry.

PERRY. It's alright. Just a career change. No big deal.

NICK. "Career change." You're a holy man, Perry. Once a holy man, always a holy man.

PERRY. You make me sound like a mystic!

(*to* **JOEL**)

It was a small Congregationalist church on the other side of town. Really, that's all it was.

NICK. *(to* **JOEL***)* He was my spiritual advisor –

PERRY. Now, don't dump that on me –

NICK. You were my spiritual advisor and you cut me loose. You cut me loose and now I am adrift!

PERRY. I…This…see, *this* really isn't fair to me!

DINK. Hey, guys –

NICK. Fair to *you?* What about me?

PERRY. What about you? This is my life! I changed jobs – so what? My God – why is this such a tremendous deal to you?

NICK. Because as long as you were a man of the cloth I had an *in*, Perry. I knew I was safe, that in times of tribulation –

PERRY. Oh, brother!

NICK. *(overlapping)* – you would put in a good word for me! You did that maybe a hundred times for me in the past and everything was fantastic, my life was great! Now you leave your calling and ever since I have been this ruined thing!

PERRY. That's not *my* fault!

NICK. You're selling fucking insurance and I am fucking adrift!

PERRY. I don't have to listen to this –

NICK. Adrift!

PERRY. I can't hear you!

NICK. *(to* **JOEL** *with great contempt)* He goes from "Put yourself in God's hands" to "Put yourself with the good hands people." Can you believe that?

DINK. *(to* **JOEL***)* Perry sells insurance now. Wichita Life and Casualty. Excellent benefits.

NICK. *(with a snort)* Insurance.

(In great frustration, PERRY shakes his fist at NICK and growls.)

Hey! Don't shake that at me!

DINK. Guys –

PERRY. *(overlapping)* Then leave me alone!

NICK. Pray for me and I will, damnitt! Come on, Perry – I need some comfort! Tell God to call off the dogs!

PERRY. Tell Him yourself!

NICK. He doesn't listen to me!

PERRY. Well He sure as hell doesn't seem to be returning *my* calls these days!

(NICK pounds PERRY on the arm.)

Ow!

JOEL. Jesus – !

DINK. *(overlapping)* Hey, fellas –

NICK. *(pounds him on the arm)* Pray for me!

PERRY. That hurts!

NICK. Pray for me, goddamitt!

JOEL. Oh, I don't believe *this*!

PERRY. Alright, alright, alright! Alright.

(NICK bows his head. A brief pause. Then...)

There.

(a beat)

NICK. What?

PERRY. I just said a prayer for you.

NICK. When?

PERRY. Just now.

NICK. When you got quiet?

PERRY. Yes. When I got quiet. Now will you drop it?

NICK. Kinda short.

PERRY. Yeah, well, I got right to the point. Alright? Please?

NICK. Well...O.K.

(A beat. Then, momentarily appeased...)

Thanks.

PERRY. *(rubbing his arm)* About crushed my arm.

(**JOEL** *has been watching in stupification. Peace restored,* **DINK** *turns to* **JOEL** *and shrugs an explanation.*)

DINK. *("Boys will be boys.")* What can you do?

PERRY. *(a weary sigh)* Jesus.

(still rubbing his arm)

So…you doing O.K., Dink?

DINK. Doin' good.

PERRY. How's Milly these days? She O.K.?

DINK. Oh, yeah, sure Perry. Thanks for asking. She's singing now, you know.

PERRY. Singing?

DINK. All the time.

NICK. Jeez…why?

DINK. Try-outs for the community theater coming up. FLOWER DRUM SONG. I've been hearing "I Enjoy Being A Girl" non-stop for the last week and a half.

*(**NICK** whistles softly.)*

NICK. She any good?

DINK. *(with a sigh)* Makes my teeth hurt. Honest to God. I went to the dentist yesterday – thought maybe I had an abscess.

*(to **JOEL**)*

Hold that will you.

(hands him something)

He couldn't even find a cavity. Finally asks me if I'm sensitive to high frequency sound? Right then I knew what was causing it. Bless her heart.

PERRY. Well, what can you do, Dink?

DINK. *(with a shrug)* She's happy as a clam.

NICK. She's the best, Dink. And you? You're a lucky man. A fortunate man. Never forget that.

DINK. I never will, Nick.

(with emotion) God knows I love that little bald-headed woman.

(**DINK**, *with great emotion, claps* **NICK** *on the back.* **PERRY** *settles in with a book and his coffee.* **NICK**, *moved, crosses away as* **JOEL** – *odd man out* – *takes it all in, still holding whatever* **DINK** *gave him. Then...*)

JOEL. Uh –

DINK. Hey, thanks a lot, Joel.

(takes it from **JOEL***)*

So, Perry – how is the new job? You doin O.K.?

PERRY. Job's fine, Dink, fine.

DINK. I talked to Milly, you know.

PERRY. Oh, no. See, Dink, you shouldn'ta done that.

DINK. Hey, come on –

PERRY. I told you not to do that.

DINK. I know you did but – what – I can't help out a pal? I just wanna help you get on your feet, Perry. That's the only reason I talked to Milly about it. That's all.

PERRY. Well, that's awful nice of you, Dink.

DINK. *(arm around* **PERRY***'s shoulder)* Hey – come on. Friends, right?

PERRY. Right.

(a beat)

So...what did Milly say?

DINK. She said "no."

PERRY. Oh.

DINK. She says we already have enough insurance.

PERRY. I see.

DINK. *(getting progressively worked up)* I told her you never got enough insurance. Just like you told me. But she still said no, Perry.

PERRY. It's alright.

DINK. God, I feel terrible about it! I tried. I pleaded with her. I begged her. I was on my knees, Perry, on my knees. You shoulda seen me. I mean, you know the kinda hold she's got on me. There was nothing I could do.

DINK. *(simply, honestly)* I'm a slave to love, Perry. You know that.

PERRY. I know – and I appreciate the effort, Dink. Besides I'm doing O.K., you know?

(JOEL *is heading for the door.*)

DINK. Hey – wait a minute –

(JOEL *stops guiltily.*)

How about Joel?

JOEL. What?

PERRY. No, Dink, please –

DINK. Have you given any thought to your insurance needs, Joel?

(pulling JOEL *back towards* **PERRY***)*

You got – what? – a wife, a coupla kids, right? Perry, come over here.

PERRY. This is really embarrassing –

DINK. What happens you walk outta here and, God forbid, calamity befalls? It could happen. Look at Walter – God rest his soul. After the grieving is over what's going to happen to your near and dear?

JOEL. We really have enough insurance.

DINK. You never got enough insurance, Joel.

JOEL. So I hear but –

DINK. Am I right, Perry?

PERRY. Dink, please.

(to JOEL*)*

Sorry. Dink tends to hover. He's a nurturer. Very in touch with his feminine side.

DINK. *(simply, honestly, and with pride)* It's true – I am.

PERRY. Always in the middle of things. Trying to make everything better no matter how impossible the situation, no matter how…how…hopeless.

(A beat. **PERRY** *has now brought himself down.)*

How very, very hopeless.

*(A pause. **DINK** sidles over to **JOEL** and, out of the side of his mouth…)*

DINK. Perry's going through a rough patch here, Joel. Do what you can, will you?

JOEL. But –

DINK. Hey, Nick – you give me a hand out here?

NICK. Yeah, O.K.

DINK. Give it some thought, Joel.

(claps him on the back.)

You're one of us now.

*(**DINK** winks at **JOEL** then exits with **NICK**.)*

JOEL. *(calling off to **DINK**)* But who *are* we?

*(Awkward pause. **JOEL** turns and smiles at **PERRY** who returns the smile. Finally…)*

Ummm –

PERRY. *(taking off his overcoat to reveal a jogging suit)* Dink's really something, isn't he?

JOEL. *(Stopping at the door. With a sigh.)* Yes. Yes he is.

PERRY. *(flapping his arms together)* He's got a heart as big as…as…

(He appears lost in thought for a moment as he continues to flap his arms. Finally…)

Well – he just has a big heart, you know?

JOEL. He seems like a nice guy.

PERRY. *(running in place)* Oh – let me tell you. He's certainly stuck with *me* through some pretty rough times. Dink and Milly – have you met Milly?

JOEL. No.

PERRY. Now *there's* a story. Remarkable woman. Anyhow – if it hadn't been for Dink and Milly, I don't know *what*. It's been that kind of year, you know what I mean?

*(**PERRY** starts stretching.)*

Yes, I…I gather that you left your church?

*(**PERRY** nods.)*

JOEL. Why...? Never mind. I'm sorry.

PERRY. It's alright. I don't mind talking about it.

JOEL. No – it's really none of my business.

PERRY. *(while he works out his neck and shoulders)* Don't worry about it. What happened was I thought I had gotten "the call" but I guess it turned out to be a wrong number. I didn't have the gift – so my congregation showed me the door.

JOEL. You were fired?

*(***PERRY** *nods as he does a couple of jumping jacks.)*

PERRY. They got together, had a meeting, took a vote. With the exception of Nick it was unanimous.

JOEL. That must of been...difficult to handle.

PERRY. Oh, well...

(He stops his exercises.)

I mean, sure – when I first got the word that my entire congregation – children and shut-ins included, for heaven's sake – had gotten together behind my back and voted to eject me from the pulpit, well, yes, certainly I was...I was –

(He is speechless. Grimacing, he shakes his fist, and makes a sound resembling a growl of exasperation. This subsides and he appears lost in thought. Finally...)

JOEL. Um...hello?

PERRY. *(In a revery. Almost to himself.)* You see, not long after Walt...well. I developed this tendency to – forget what I was praying about. My mind would wander. One Sunday while I was giving the benediction, I paused, and, for some reason, I started thinking about fishing on Lake Erie, being all alone, and floating in my boat. Just floating. Floating away from...everything. The sun warming my face, the wind softly blowing, the boat gently rocking as it rode the swells. Up and down. Up and down.

(A sigh. A beat.)

Up and down. Quiet and…at peace. No pain, no constant, yammering complaints, no problems. Nothing.

(Long pause. Not knowing what else to do, **JOEL** *loudly clears his voice.* **PERRY** *shakes himself out of his revery.)*

My wife later told me I'd paused in mid-sentence for maybe a minute and a half. A minute and a half of absolute silence.

(musing)

Probably the most profound thing that ever happened in my church. Anyway, when I came out of it, the congregation had left in boredom and disgust. That night they voted to fire me. So before they could fire me, I quit.

*(**PERRY** turns and sees **JOEL** looking at him. This seems to bring him to. An embarrassed laugh of explanation.)*

Pride.

(a beat)

Well…what is in the past, is in the past. Things work out for the best and…well – if you happen to change your mind about…

(A beat. Another embarrassed laugh.)

– about the – you know – insurance, here's my card.

JOEL. *(with a resigned sigh)* Thanks.

*(**DINK** and **NICK** enter carrying a heavy trunk of some sort.)*

DINK. Comin' through, comin' through!

*(**JOEL** is startled and shouts.)*

NICK. Jesus, pal!

JOEL. Oh –

*(**JOEL** backs up but remains in the way of **NICK** and **DINK** as they careen towards him.)*

NICK. Gang way!

JOEL. *(still backing)* Sorry –

(NICK *and* DINK *continue stumbling towards* JOEL.)

NICK. I'm goin to pop a testicle you don't get the hell outta the way!

(JOEL *is backed to the wall.* NICK *and* DINK *drop the trunk just in front of the cringing* JOEL *and collapse, panting on the trunk.*)

Jesus wept!

PERRY. *(crossing to* JOEL*)* Are you alright, Joel?

JOEL. I'm fine, I'm fine.

NICK. Jesus – !

DINK. *(Delighted, clapping his hands together.)* Hey – look at you two! Making friends, huh? That's great.

PERRY. Getting acquainted, Dink.

DINK. That's great.

PERRY. He's a great guy.

DINK. Oh, he is – no question. Hey, Perry – I was looking for the cards awhile ago. You see 'em?

PERRY. I'll help you find them.

(PERRY *crosses over to help* DINK *find the cards. Before he exits, he turns back to* JOEL.)

Joel – thanks for…you know. Just listening. Sometimes it's good to have a sympathetic ear.

(PERRY *exits.* DINK *turns to* JOEL *and gives him a big "thumbs up." He waits expectantly until* JOEL *hesitantly returns the gesture.* DINK *exits.*)

(JOEL *stands in the middle of the room for a moment, utterly confused. He finally turns to find* NICK *looking at him intently. An awkward pause. Then…*)

NICK. What were you guys talking about?

JOEL. Just…you know. Things.

(A beat. Then…)

NICK. That's Walt's hat.

JOEL. Yes. I –

NICK. You're wearing Walt's hat.

JOEL. *(weakly)* Dink gave it to me.

(a brief pause)

NICK. Right.

(a beat)

Alright. Gimme a hand with this, willya pal?

JOEL. I'm sorry – what?

NICK. Grab that end over there.

JOEL. *(picking up end of the board)* Uh…Excuse me but is *this* what we're doing?

NICK. What?

JOEL. Is this some kind of renovation project?

NICK. I just wanta fix this, alright? Now come on. Stand up on this thing.

JOEL. *(stepping up on the trunk)* But is this what we're doing here? Because, the thing is…I'm not handy.

NICK. What?

JOEL. I'm not a handy man. I'm not comfortable working with my hands.

NICK. Who cares? I just want you to hold the board!

JOEL. But I didn't come dressed for construction –

NICK. Hey, listen – I don't know you but around here? We pitch in, we help each other out, we lend a hand, you hear what I'm saying?

JOEL. I hear you but –

NICK. You hear what I'm saying?

JOEL. Yes.

NICK. Now – just hold it here like this, O.K.?

JOEL. O.K.

NICK. O.K.! Jesus.

*(**JOEL** ends up holding the board in an awkward position over his head. **NICK** gets his hammer, nails, and work apron.)*

JOEL. I'm sorry. Obviously I misunderstood Leo. I didn't come prepared to work. I'm sorry.

NICK. Ah, shit.

(Hefting his hammer. A pause.)

Hey, look – I'm the one who oughta apologize. I'm outta control, pal. I been jumpin' all over people left and right. I mean, lately, I been kinda nuts.

JOEL. *(apprehensively eyeing* **NICK***'s hammer)* Really?

NICK. See…things ain't so good right now, you know? Tell you the truth – things don't pick up I'm in a desperate situation.

JOEL. Oh.

NICK. A little higher there, pal.

*(***JOEL*** valiantly tries holding the board higher.)*

I mean, I'm not afraid of hard work, you hear me?

JOEL. Yes.

NICK. A man hires me to do a job? He owns me. I'm his mule. I'm not afraid of hard work. I bust my ass is what I do, pal. A days work for a days pay. Everybody in town knows *that*.

JOEL. *(straining)* Uh-huh –

NICK. So what happens? I find out I don't get the contract for this job here even though I know for a fact I bid it lower than anybody in town. Contractors I bust my ass for the past 10 years, suddenly they can't use me. I can't get no work! And you know why?

JOEL. *(with difficulty)* No.

NICK. 'Cause Buck Drum sits on his crapper and falls through his fuckin floor. That's why.

JOEL. *(a realization)* What?! Buck Drum – ?

NICK. Yeah. You know him?

JOEL. Well –

NICK. Bastard. So what I put the bathroom floor in the day before – that make it my fault?

JOEL. *(almost a moan)* Oh my God –

NICK. What – you never heard of defective plywood? It could happen to anybody.

(**JOEL** *lets the board slip.*)

Hold it still, pal!

(**JOEL** *lifts the board again and* **NICK** *continues.*)

JOEL. Sorry.

NICK. Fallin' through the floor with his pants around his ankles musta made Buck kinda irrational cause the bastard calls me, says "You hammered your last nail in this town, asshole." He puts the word out – all of a sudden, I can't even get crew work. Goes on to tell me he's got some hotshot lawyer just moved into town workin for him.

JOEL. (*miserably*) Oh no –

NICK. Yeah – this bloodsucker's gonna sue me for a quarter million dollars! 250 grand, you believe that?

JOEL. (*to himself*) Shit.

NICK. Exactly. He breaks his leg cause of an act a God and he sues *me*. What a fuckin country lawyers, right?

JOEL. (*weakly*) Right.

NICK. (*hammers the board or something*) You can let go now, pal. Anyhow…sure as hell hope Leo can do something cause I'm all outta ideas.

(**DINK** *and* **PERRY** *re-enter.*)

DINK. (*happily holding up the cards*) Found 'em!

(**NICK** *reaches for something near* **JOEL**. *At this,* **JOEL** *flinches mightily, throwing his arms up as if protecting his face.*)

JOEL. Auuughhh!

NICK. Jesus!

DINK. Holy cow! Nicky, what did you do?

NICK. I didn't do nothin! I was just reaching for my jacket –

PERRY. Are you alright, Joel?

JOEL. I'm fine –

NICK. – I wasn't going to deck him!

JOEL. I know. I…I just have a highly developed flinch reflex.

NICK. No shit.

JOEL. I tend to over-react when I feel threatened. I don't have any control over it. It's kind of embarrassing.

NICK. *(under his breath to* **PERRY***)* It's kinda weird.

DINK. Joel, you don't feel threatened by *us*, do you?

JOEL. Well –

DINK. Because we're delighted you're joining us, right guys?

NICK. Sure.

PERRY. Absolutely.

JOEL. Yes, yes, that's very kind of you but –

(**NICK** *has sidled up beside* **JOEL** *and now makes another quick movement. Once again,* **JOEL** *flinches mightily and shouts out.*)

NICK. *(with a laugh)* That's great.

JOEL. Please!

NICK. I'm sorry, pal. I'm sorry.

(**NICK** *makes another quick movement at* **JOEL** *who flinches.* **NICK** *is really enjoying himself. With a laugh.*)

Terrific.

PERRY. *(smiling)* Come on, Nick, give him a break.

NICK. Why do you do that? Some kinda condition or something?

JOEL. *(testily)* It's not a "condition."

NICK. O.K. Whatever.

JOEL. It's not a "condition." It's something I've had since I was a child but it is not a "condition."

NICK. Hey, I don't know you – and no offense – but that's screwy.

JOEL. I'm simply a bit jumpy, that's all. I have recently moved to town, I'm new to this little club or…group or…whatever, and I've been trying very hard to assimilate –

NICK. Do what?

JOEL. – but it's difficult. I'm on edge. Anyone would be.

DINK. Relax. You're among friends here, Joel. We're pals.

JOEL. *(vexed)* But we don't know each other!

DINK. You're our pal. Nick, tell him he's our pal.

NICK. Let me tell you something – you come in this room? Far as I'm concerned, you're a pal.

(Flicks his hand at **JOEL** *who, once again, flinches mightily.)*

PERRY. Come on!

DINK. Nick!

NICK. *(laughing)* Sca – rewy!

JOEL. Stop it, alright?

PERRY. Hey, Nick –

NICK. Alright, alright.

PERRY. Don't let Nick get to you. He just likes to pick.

DINK. *(with a shrug as he shuffles his cards)* He's a trickster, Joel.

PERRY. He doesn't mean anything.

DINK. He's irrepressible.

(then, pleasantly)

Would you like to play some cards, Joel? A nice, relaxing game of rummy maybe?

JOEL. No. No thank you. No. I –

(An awkward pause. Finally…)

Look. Fellows, it was nice meeting you but I need to be running along.

DINK. You're taking off?

PERRY. Why?

NICK. Shit. It was what I did, wasn't it? You know – with the –

(He flicks his hand at **JOEL** *who flinches.)*

Hey, come on, pal – I'm sorry. I was just screwing around.

PERRY. He was just screwing around.

NICK. Blowin' off some steam. I told you – things haven't been goin too good for me lately. I hadta vent. You understand.

PERRY. You understand?

JOEL. Perfectly understandable but I need to be going –

DINK. Leo's going to be very disappointed, Joel. Heartbroken, right guys?

PERRY. Crestfallen.

NICK. He's been very low lately, pal. Very low. See, I don't know if anyone told you about Walter or not.

DINK. *(raising his hand)* I did.

JOEL. Yes, well, give Leo my regrets but –

DINK. Leo was so delighted you were going to be joining us. Happier than I seen him in almost a year.

NICK. Happier than he's been since old Walt kicked the bucket, I'll tell you that.

DINK. Just thinking about you joining us? Quite frankly, Joel, I think maybe that gave Leo the strength to continue.

JOEL. That's insane! We only met the one time! We talked for maybe five minutes. That's all!

PERRY. Leo's a great judge of character. Sometimes all it takes is five minutes.

DINK. I know Leo thinks it's important you're here, Joel.

(As if hearing something far in the distance, **NICK** *freezes.)*

JOEL. But he never said what he wanted me to do! The man communicated in a series of coughs, belches, chuckles and endearments!

PERRY. That's our Leo.

NICK. *(softly)* Wait a minute…

*(***NICK*** stands very still as if hearing – or maybe sensing – something.)*

JOEL. Yes, no doubt he's a very sweet man but the fact remains I do not know why I am here and that makes me tremendously uncomfortable! I simply am not the sort who can blindly enter into any kind of relationship based merely upon the assurances of an avuncular total stranger! I am not a spontaneous person!

(DINK leads JOEL to a chair where he sits.)

DINK. Come on – he'll be here soon. Have a seat – would you like a soda?

JOEL. No!

DINK. Some nice cold soda?

JOEL. Please –

(PERRY crosses to the other side of JOEL's chair.)

PERRY. Maybe some coffee? Some nice hot coffee?

NICK. *(still looking out)* Guys –

JOEL. No thank you! Now, please – I must be going.

NICK. *(louder)* Hey! Hey! Hey!

(JOEL and PERRY stop and turn towards NICK. They take a few steps away from JOEL.)

JOEL. What? Wha…what is it?

(The three men face different directions as if listening to some distant sound. Silence.)

DINK. *(softly)* Leo.

NICK. *(softly)* Leo.

JOEL. *(straining to hear)* I don't…I don't hear anything.

(Pause as he gets very still and listens to the silence.)

What?

PERRY. *(softly)* Leo.

(A beat as JOEL looks at the guys standing in the silence. Then…)

JOEL. Oh, well, this is ridiculous.

(crossing to get his briefcase)

Gentlemen, it has been a pleasure. I'm sorry I have to leave but under the circumstances I'm sure you will –

(JOEL is starting for the door when LEO APPLEGATE bursts in, carrying a Taco Bell bag.)

LEO. Boys!

NICK. Leo!

DINK. *(to JOEL)* See?

JOEL. How did – ?

PERRY. *(overlapping)* Great to see you, Leo!

DINK. *(beaming and vigorously shaking LEO's hand)* Hiya, Leo.

LEO. How you doin', grandpa?

DINK. *(to JOEL. Absolutely delighted.)* You see?

> *(back to LEO)*
>
> I'm doing great, Leo. Just great.

JOEL. But I didn't hear anything. How – ?

LEO. Nicky.

NICK. How's it goin', Leo?

LEO. Nicky.

NICK. Yeah – I know, Leo.

LEO. You hangin' in there?

NICK. *(with a shrug)* I'm hangin' in there.

> *(LEO looks at him closely for a moment.)*

LEO. Alright.

> *(Sees PERRY. A beat.)*
>
> And *you*.

PERRY. *(nervously)* Hello, Leo.

> *(Pause, then LEO holds out his arms.)*

LEO. Come here you.

> *(PERRY walks over and into LEO's embrace.)*

DINK. *(almost tearing up)* Ah, look at that. Isn't that terrific?

LEO. You do what's right for you? I got no problems.

PERRY. *(with emotion)* Thanks. Thanks, Leo.

LEO. Just remember that.

> *(LEO heads for the table, carrying his Taco Bell bag.)*

DINK. Little snack, Leo?

LEO. Hey, I tellya what, Dink – they oughta just save time, cut open my chest, and wrap this thing around my heart. But what the hell – I love the stuff, Dink.

DINK. Me too. Milly doesn't like me eating there – she's worried I get the cholesterol, you know – but I sneak one every once in awhile.

(**JOEL** *clears his throat.*)

LEO. *(Turning, he sees* **JOEL** *and crosses to shake his hand.)* Well...hey, hey – there he is!

JOEL. Yes indeed.

(**LEO** *puts his hands on* **JOEL***'s shoulders and looks at him closely.*)

LEO. Here you are.

(An awkward moment)

JOEL. What? What is it?

LEO. *(A beat, then...)* Hey, look, pardon me, Joel – you live alone, you eat what you like, when you feel like it. You want a nacho or something?

JOEL. No thank you.

LEO. I usually get fries and a burger over at Burger King but I figured life's short. You sure you don't want a nacho, Joel?

JOEL. No thanks. I –

LEO. Anybody else? Perry? Nicky? Nacho?

NICK. Nah.

LEO. Sure?

NICK. I'm sure.

LEO. Come on – a nacho, a little of this cream? Can't beat it with a stick.

NICK. Ate before I got here, Leo.

LEO. Where you eat?

NICK. Pizza Hut.

LEO. How 'bout that? I ate buffet there last night.

NICK. Yeah?

LEO. The salad bar, huh?

(Finishes slurping his soda.)

NICK. They got a good salad bar there, Leo.

LEO. Not a bad salad bar – get me a pop, willya Perry?

(PERRY goes for a soda.)

– not a bad salad bar but in my opinion not as good as Eat'n Park.

DINK. Eat'n Park's got a good salad bar, Leo.

LEO. Me and Walt used to go to Eat'n Park once, twice a week just for the salad. You a salad man, Joel?

JOEL. Well, yes, I suppose I –

(PERRY re-enters with a soda.)

LEO. Me? I like mostly the lettuce, buncha that shredded cheese, croutons, bacon bits, maybe, every once in awhile, a coupla those little midget carrots, you know what I mean?

PERRY. *(handing soda to LEO)* Here you go, Leo.

LEO. Walt, though – thanks, kid – Walt, he'd get all *that* plus 4, maybe 5 slices of tomato, a handful of cukes –

(takes a big gulp of soda then continues almost without stopping)

LEO. *(cont.)* – hard-boiled eggs, those crunchy noodles, a big blobba jello, beets, buncha buffalo wings, 3 or 4 packs of crackers, a coupla –

(He stops – in some discomfort.)

PERRY. Leo – you O.K.?

(LEO nods, indicates "wait a minute" by holding up his hand and, after a moment, belches and continues.)

LEO. – a coupla slabs a butter on the side. He'd mix it all together and then, after he had this great, big pile of good things to eat? He'd pour a low-fat dressing over the top. Said he needed to watch his diet.

(laughing)

That was Walter.

DINK. The man loved his salad, Leo. No question of it.
LEO. Good old Walter.
NICK. He was a pisser.
LEO. He was. He was a pisser. He was that.

(Brief pause. Then, with emotion.)

Kee-ripes – I miss him, boys.
NICK. *(with a big sigh)* Yeah. Me too.
PERRY. Old Walt.
DINK. I think we all miss him, Leo.

*(All murmur agreement except, naturally, **JOEL**. **DINK** gets **JOEL**'s attention and motions for him to agree.)*

JOEL. But I didn't….

*(a warning glare from **NICK** who also motions to **LEO**)*

Sure.
LEO. A man like Walt comes around only once in a lifetime.

*(puts his arm around **JOEL**'s shoulder)*

He was a rare individual, Joel.
JOEL. *(very uncomfortable)* I see.
LEO. I tell you one thing, boys – it's been one hell of a year. Much has happened to each one of us on this journey through life we share. Many bumps along the way. But…we're here, right boys? We're here and as long as we're together, old Walt'll be right here with us.

*(Tremendously moved, **DINK** embraces **LEO**, and stands linked with **LEO** and the uncomfortable **JOEL**. **LEO** is misting up.)*

Welcome, Joel.
JOEL. *(weakly)* Thank you.
LEO. If you don't mind, guys, I'd like for us to offer up a prayer in Walt's memory. Perry?
PERRY. *(A deer caught in the head-lights.)* Huh?
LEO. Lead us in prayer for Walt, willya?

(DINK, LEO, *and* NICK *bow their heads.* JOEL *is flabbergasted but, after a moment, bows his head. There is a long pause.*)

LEO. Perry?

PERRY. I...I'm not sure I can do that, Leo.

LEO. What?

PERRY. I can't.

LEO. Sure you can.

DINK. We won't tell nobody.

NICK. Screw the church.

DINK. Yeah – screw 'em.

LEO. Perry – anybody can pray.

PERRY. Not me.

LEO. Kee-ripes, you're a private citizen. A free agent. You can pray till the cows come home.

PERRY. (*miserably*) You don't understand. It's not that. I'm sorry.

NICK. (*hissing – head still bowed*) You gotta do it, Perry. For Walter.

PERRY. I can't.

NICK. (*shoving him*) Do it!

DINK. Hey –

PERRY. Don't push!

NICK. (*pounding him on the arm*) Do it!

PERRY. (*a cry*) Dear God!

(*The guys all bow their heads. A beat. Then, a sigh.*)

Dear God...

(*Pause. He bows his head.*)

Dear God. Sometimes as we...go through our...well –

(*A pause. The others shift position, clear their throats.* JOEL *lifts his head and looks at the panicking* PERRY. *Finally...*)

As we go through our lives we...

*(A pause as **PERRY** fights for inspiration. His eyes are tightly closed and his face shows the strain of trying to maintain his train of thought.)*

You see, our dear friend Walter Deagon…Old Walt… Walt…

*(A long pause. **PERRY** is "off." Finally, **DINK** crosses next to **PERRY**.)*

DINK. Dink here, God. I'm the guy Walter died on top of. Anyhow, I think what Perry is trying to say, God, is that we really miss old Walt and we want you to keep him in your thoughts just like…well – just like we do. That's all. In your name. Amen.

(The men all mutter "amen.")

LEO. Amen. Thanks, Dink. That was terrific.
DINK. Sure.

*(**DINK** sits at the table and begins to play solitaire.)*

NICK. Jesus Christ, Perry –
PERRY. *(picks up his book)* Leave me alone, please.
NICK. I mean, Jesus Christ. I ain't much of a Christian but Jesus Christ!
PERRY. *(trying to read)* I know!
NICK. That was piss poor!
PERRY. Don't blame me! I told you I couldn't do it.
NICK. I hope to hell you prayed better than that for *me!*
PERRY. Oh please – !
NICK. You didn't do a better job than *that* I am screwed!

*(**PERRY** again growls and shakes his fist at **NICK**.)*

Damnit, will you stop that?

LEO. Hey, Nicky – ease up. Dink picked up the ball. The word got through. No problem, right?
NICK. Yeah. I guess.

*(**NICK** sulks off. A brief pause. Seizing the moment, **JOEL** crosses to **LEO**.)*

JOEL. Excuse me, Leo –

LEO. *(reflective)* The great circle. Right, Joel?

JOEL. Huh?

LEO. The great circle.

> *(sitting and offering JOEL a seat)*
>
> We've been together for – Kee-ripes, I don't know how long. Years and years, right Dink?

DINK. *(as he deals out another solitaire hand)* I started coming right after my gall bladder. That's gotta be 10, maybe 12 years. You and Walter were even earlier than me.

LEO. Walt met you in the hospital!

DINK. Yeah, that's right. Asked me if I wanted to drop by after I got back on my feet. He was doin' that volunteer work at the time, remember?

LEO. Worked the information desk – sure. Volunteered, Joel. As busy as Walt was, he still found time to volunteer. That's the kinda man Walt was. That was Walt.

DINK. I dropped by the first day I'm outta the hospital and I been comin ever since.

LEO. Comradery, Joel.

> *(eating)*
>
> I'm telling you – my hand to the Bible –
>
> *(offering some of his food to JOEL, practically sticking it in his face)*
>
> You sure you don't want some?
>
> **(JOEL** *shakes his head.* **LEO** *takes a bite and continues.)*
>
> – if wasn't for these guys here? I don't know how I woulda made it through the past year.
>
> *(reflecting)*
>
> I mean, there were times, Joel.
>
> *(A beat. Quietly.)*
>
> There were times.
>
> *(He belches.)*
>
> God this is good.

(Offers **JOEL** *some nachos.* **JOEL** *shakes his head.)*

JOEL. Leo, I've been trying to find out from your friends –

LEO. Great buncha guys, aren't they?

JOEL. Everyone's been very nice –

LEO. They really seem to have taken a shine to *you*, lemme tell you.

JOEL. Yes, well, frankly, I find that odd.

LEO. Odd?

JOEL. *(wryly)* I'm not used to unconditional acceptance.

LEO. You're kidding. Why?

JOEL. Leo –

(looks around for **NICK***)*

I'm a lawyer.

LEO. *(with a laugh)* But you're one of the guys!

JOEL. No, Leo – I'm not.

LEO. You're being too hard on yourself.

JOEL. You misunderstand. It doesn't bother me. I don't care. I have never been one of the guys.

LEO. Never?

JOEL. Never. I have never *aspired* to be one of the guys. On the contrary, I have always wanted to be *apart* from the guys! I've never hung out, I've never shot the breeze, I've never goofed off –

LEO. What're you talking? Everybody goofs off.

JOEL. Not me. Everything has to have a purpose.

LEO. So why're you here?

(a beat)

JOEL. That's what I want to know! Other than the fact that you invited me, why am I here?

*(***LEO** *smiles enigmatically.)*

LEO. I invited you?

JOEL. Leo!

(A pause as **LEO** *stands and puts his arm around* **JOEL***'s shoulders. First a belch then…)*

LEO. You ever notice how similar our names are? Like except for the "J" Joel is Leo backwards?

(a beat)

JOEL. *(flabbergasted)* What?! Is that – ? *What?*

LEO. Just thought it was interesting.

(offers him some nachos)

You sure you don't want some of this?

JOEL. Leo…why am I here?

LEO. Walt died.

(to **DINK***)*

Red 7 on the 8. We had an opening.

JOEL. Yes. Yes, I understand that but why me? How do I fit in?

LEO. Let's just say a man in your field brings some…unique talents to the group.

(to **DINK***)*

2 on the 3. Never know when we might have to call on you.

JOEL. What are you talking about?

LEO. *(with a wink)* You know.

(to **DINK***)*

The 3.

DINK. What?

JOEL. Wait a minute!

LEO. *(pointing)* The 3.

DINK. Oh!

JOEL. You said this group's activities were not illegal.

LEO. Strictly speaking, they're not.

JOEL. Whoa. Whoa, wait a minute, Leo, I believe I should inform you right now that I am not interested in anything which smacks of illegality.

LEO. *(points to a move)* 10.

DINK. The 10! Thanks.

JOEL. Leo!

LEO. Joel, relax. I'm just yankin your chain.

JOEL. You...wait a minute – you mean you're kidding?

DINK. *(with a laugh)* He's got a great sense of humor, doesn't he, Leo?

LEO. Oh, he's a terrific sport.

JOEL. Then if you're kidding just what – ?

LEO. Joel, don't worry about it. Everything will become clear.

JOEL. But –

LEO. Great having you with us, kid.

*(**LEO** crosses over to **NICK** as **PERRY** walks over to **JOEL**.)*

JOEL. Leo!

PERRY. He's really something, isn't he? The way he can come into a room and instantly make everyone feel better. More alive. Safer somehow. If I had maybe an ounce of that optimism, that joy of living, maybe I wouldn't have...

(a beat)

God – he's a great man, Joel.

JOEL. Perry, what's going on here? I feel like I've been kidnapped by some tremendously bizarre cult, honest to God I do. What's going on?

PERRY. What?

JOEL. Why am I here?

PERRY. Oh no. Please – don't. Don't ask me that.

JOEL. No one else will give me a straight answer! I've been here half an hour and I know less now than I did when I came in! It's a simple question.

PERRY. Please –

JOEL. *(grabbing him by the shoulders)* Why am I here?

PERRY. Well...now, alright, see, the problem I have is when you ask "Why am I here?" do you mean "Why am I here in this room" or...or...

(He gestures to all of creation.)

"Why am I *here*?

JOEL. Why am I here *now*! *Here* in this particular place, at this particular point in time!

PERRY. Oh. Ohhhh! Whew…that's a relief. *That* I can answer.

JOEL. Finally!

PERRY. The other one? God. That's the one I used to hear all the time. "Why am I here, Reverend? Why am I here? Why?"

JOEL. Perry – ?

PERRY. You'd be surprised how often I used to hear that question. Why does God do this, why does God do that. Why do I have to suffer, why do I have to die? Why does God allow such…such terrible, terrible things to happen? Why?

JOEL. Perry – please stay on the subject!

PERRY. Everyone was always looking to me, wanting – no – demanding answers. But I couldn't answer them, Joel. I'd search and search my heart for answers but I'd get so lost inside myself I couldn't speak. I couldn't…I just couldn't –

(He's starting to "drift off" again.)

JOEL. Perry!

PERRY. I don't know why we're here. We just are and sometimes it hurts. It hurts badly. That's it.

JOEL. Perry!

*(**PERRY** is "off" and wanders away. **LEO** grabs the deck of cards and loudly ruffles them.)*

LEO. O.K. So whaddya say, boys? Whaddya say?

DINK. Sure, Leo.

NICK. *(crossing to the table)* Yeah. O.K.

LEO. Perry?

*(**PERRY** continues to be lost in his thoughts. Louder.)*

Perry?

*(**NICK** pops **PERRY** one on the back of his head.)*

PERRY. Ow!

(**PERRY** *again growls and shakes his fist at* **NICK.**)

NICK. Hey! Don't shake that thing at me unless you intend to use it!

DINK. Guys –

NICK. I'll tell you something, Perry – it's beginning to piss me off.

LEO. Come on, boys –

NICK. He keeps doing it at me, Leo. I do anything he shakes his fist at me.

PERRY. It's just a…a gesture. It doesn't hurt anybody.

NICK. Try being on the receiving end of that thing!

PERRY. Oh, please –

DINK. Mr. Coppopolus! *That's* who it is! I been racking my brains.

(*a beat*)

PERRY. What?

DINK. Ran a fruit stand in my neighborhood when I was a kid. You do that you remind me of Mr. Coppopolus.

PERRY. Oh.

DINK. (*dealing out another solitaire hand*) Yeah, see, me and my brother – we used to pinch fruit from him. You know – grab a apple, coupla pears, maybe a cantalope they're in season. Nothin big but – Christ on a bike! You think we stole his eyes he'd get so upset. We'd go maybe half-way down the block, turn around, and just stand there eatin and laughin at Mr. Coppopolus. He'd sputter and blubber and finally, just when you thought he'd have a stroke he'd throw up this scrawny little arm with this knobby little fist on the end of it and shake it like it was this horrible weapon or something and yell "Damn kids," tears just streamin down his face. And we'd laugh – honest to God, sometimes we'd laugh so hard you'd feel like you were bleedin from the ears.

PERRY. You were stealing the old man's fruit. Why'd you laugh at him?

DINK. 'Cause we knew all he'd ever do was shake his fist at us. He never called the cops, he never chased us. He just waved that boney little arm. It was all just kinda…I don't know –

NICK. Irritating?

DINK. Oh, no. Kinda –

NICK. Stupid?

DINK. No –

JOEL. Pathetic?

PERRY. Hey!

DINK. Yeah. Yeah – now that you mention it, it *was* kinda pathetic. Pathetic and pitiful and kinda heartbreaking.

(a beat)

PERRY. *(crosses away with his book)* Gee – thanks, Dink.

DINK. Oh. Oh – Christ on a bike, Perry, I didn't mean you were…well, you know.

NICK. Adrift, Perry. Adrift.

(DINK pats PERRY on the back then crosses to the table.)

LEO. Hey, Perry?

(PERRY turns to LEO.)

Hang in there.

PERRY. Yeah. Yeah, O.K.

LEO. So whaddya say – a little hearts?

PERRY. *(with a sigh)* Alright.

(PERRY crosses to the table.)

NICK. *(sitting)* Thought we were playing rummy.

LEO. Whatever. How about it, Joel? Maybe some rummy?

DINK. Yeah, whaddya say?

NICK. Park it, pal.

PERRY. Have a seat.

JOEL. Wait a minute, wait a minute!

(A beat. Then…)

Is *this* why you invited me? Just to play cards? Is this just…some kind of a *card* club?

(The guys all laugh good-naturedly.)

Because I'm not a card player, Leo. I don't play at all. Really. I never play.

(The guys laugh.)

Is that what we're doing here?

(No answer as the laughter continues.)

What? What?

LEO. Joel, that's what we're doing but that's not why we're here.

JOEL. What?

LEO. You're a busy man. We wouldn't have you drop everything just to come here to play cards. Now – have a seat and let's play some cards.

JOEL. No thank you.

LEO. Come on – it's hearts –

NICK. Thought it was rummy.

LEO. – it's rummy. It's not hard. We'll teach you as we go. Cut 'em, Perry.

*(**PERRY** does so.)*

JOEL. But –

DINK. It's a wonderful game, Joel.

JOEL. Please – I really, really have to be getting along. Really.

LEO. *(dealing)* Now, everyone gets seven cards –

JOEL. You see…well – my wife –

PERRY. Dealer gets eight.

LEO. Right.

JOEL. *(sitting)* I see. Anyway, my wife –

NICK. So you're married, huh?
DINK. *(to* **JOEL***)* You try to make books –
JOEL. *(to* **NICK***)* Excuse me?
DINK. – you know – three or four of a kind?
NICK. I said "You married?"
LEO. *(holding nacho to* **PERRY***)* You sure?

(**PERRY** *shakes his head "no."*)

JOEL. Wha...? Yes. Yes, I am and I told my wife I wasn't going to be very long because –
DINK. You take one from the stack –
JOEL. – you see, she asked –
PERRY. Then you discard what you don't want.
JOEL. – you know – how long I was going to be and –
DINK. See?
JOEL. Uh...yes. Very good. And I told her I...I wasn't going to be very long –
DINK. *(happily)* There's nothing to it.
LEO. It's a terrific game.
NICK. We playin' a penny a point?
PERRY. Just a couple of hands, Joel.
DINK. It'll be fun.
JOEL. As I said my wife is expecting me –
NICK. So your wife wants you home, huh?

(picking up a card)

I got that.

JOEL. *(a testy sigh)* Yes. Yes she does.
NICK. *(a noncommital grunt)* Hmm.
JOEL. Now...now what's that supposed to mean?
NICK. Nothing.
LEO. Now we're goin', now we're goin'.

(The guys continue to play.)

NICK. So – you just move to town, huh?
JOEL. Yes.

DINK. They live over on Poplar Street, Nick.

(**NICK** *whistles.*)

NICK. Nice neighborhood. So, what? You buy or what?

JOEL. Well, it's —

LEO. Discard.

JOEL. Sorry.

(*He discards.*)

We bought an older place —

NICK. A fix'er up?

JOEL. Well —

NICK. Then, hey, keep me in mind, you know what I'm saying? 'Cause I do renovations! Sure! I mean, shit — I did old Walt's cellar, idn't that right, Leo? Turned it into this kinda den or something. I thought it turned out pretty good, right guys?

(*An uncomfortable beat. Finally…*)

LEO. Your play, kid.

NICK. (*discarding*) So keep me in mind, O.K.?

PERRY. (*picking up a card*) I'll take that.

DINK. You dirty dog.

NICK. So, pal, whaddya do anyway?

JOEL. Do? Uh…well…a variety of things. I'm involved in a…a variety of things. I…

(*Nervously clearing his throat.*)

Well, for one thing I'm a classical music enthusiast.

NICK. No, I mean, whaddya do for a living?

JOEL. (*nervously*) Hmmm?

LEO. Joel?

JOEL. Hmmm?

DINK. I think it's your play, Joel.

PERRY. You need to discard one.

(**JOEL** *discards and* **NICK** *picks it up.*)

NICK. Hey — that's mine.

DINK. How long you been married, Joel?
JOEL. Uhhh...15 years. No. 14. 14, 15 years. I don't...
NICK. Wait a minute. 14, 15 – what – you don't know?
JOEL. Yes, of course I know. It's 15.

(beat)

14.

NICK. Right. Listen, pal, lemme tell you what. I don't know you from Adam but a word to the wise – watch yourself, you know what I'm sayin?
JOEL. No.
NICK. You may think things are fine? Next thing you know you ruin your life and you end up this worthless thing.
DINK. Oh, Nicky –
NICK. Don't lose the magic, alright? I don't care what –
LEO. Think you probably needta discard again there, Joel.
NICK. *(leaning into JOEL)* You hear what I'm saying to you?
JOEL. *(recoiling)* Yes, yes I do. Please –
NICK. Keep the magic!

(picking up JOEL's discard)

I'll take that nine.

LEO. You workin on nines are you, Nicky?

(a beat)

DINK. *(getting his wallet out)* Hey, Joel – wanna see my bride? That's what I call her. Been married almost 30 years and I still call her my bride.

(with a laugh)

Cracks her up.

(DINK gives JOEL the picture.)

LEO. Milly's got one of those laughs.
NICK. No shit. Let me tell you something, pal – once she gets going...?
PERRY. *(with a laugh)* Yeah.

(a beat)

JOEL. *(looking at the picture)* That's…um…Pirates, isn't it?

DINK. That's her favorite cap. Been wearing it for years. She used to wear these wigs? Holy cow! I didn't care much for 'em. Looked like a hair hat, you know? I said what's the point? You wear something like that everyone knows you're bald anyway so what the hell? Mostly now she just wears this old Pirates cap. She's a big fan.

(A beat. Looking at the picture with great love.)

Idn't she great?

JOEL. Yes. She has a…a nice smile.

DINK. You know, Joel, to this day, every so often she'll give me that smile? I'm 20 years old again and putty in her hands.

JOEL. *(sincerely)* Thanks for letting me see her picture.

DINK. *(putting the picture back in his wallet)* Pleasure's all mine, Joel.

LEO. So the Mrs.' doin O.K., Dink?

DINK. Ah, you know – she has her good days, she has her bad days.

(to JOEL)

She acts a little goofy sometimes, that's all. Chemicals or something.

PERRY. *(A quiet explanation to JOEL.)* Alzheimers.

DINK. Yeah. She'll be alright, though.

(almost as an afterthought)

She's goin to be in a musical, you know.

NICK. Hear that, pal? Magic.

LEO. *(to JOEL)* You know, when Nicky's right, he's right – and he's right. I mean, what Milly and Dink have? Joel, after 14 or 15 years, you gotta feel it yourself.

JOEL. Excuse me?

LEO. With…you know.

(Beat. JOEL is lost.)

Your wife?

JOEL. Oh. Monica.

> *(with just the slightest hesitation)*

Right.

LEO. Well, then, there you go, you know what I'm saying. To have a companion – don't matter who – but to have a *companion*, someone to travel beside you, to help get through it all? That does not come along every day. Mark my words. It does not.

JOEL. I see.

LEO. Now Walt, Joel…Walter –

> *(takes a quick gulp of pop)*

Walt understood this, am I right guys?

DINK. He had it figured out, Leo.

LEO. Give you an example –

> *(another quick sip)*

Walt had this dog, this little chihuahua, Joel. Kee-ripes – did Walt love that little guy!

DINK. Randy.

LEO. Called him Randy. Walter used to dress him up like he was a little friend. You know what I'm sayin? Started off when he bought this little red dog sweater from the pet store. You know – so Randy wouldn't get cold in the wintertime when Walt took him out to pee and do his little "doody."

JOEL. "Doody?"

LEO. Yeah…you know.

DINK. *(rather delicately)* His "business," Joel.

JOEL. Oh.

LEO. Well, Walt liked the way Randy looked in that sweater so much, he got him this little pair of blue jeans, a coupla pairs of these tiny little sequined cowboy boots – even bought him a little toupee.

JOEL. What?

LEO. My hand to the Bible. Randy wore a toupee.

DINK. That was one cute dog.

LEO. Oh, he was a rascal that one! He'd take no crap offa anybody – I don't care how big. You cross Randy and he'd bark so hard his toupee would fall over his eyes.

DINK. Christ on a bike, that little guy had an attitude, didn't he?

LEO. Loaded with personality. Me and Walt and Randy used to take walks in the park along the river. Oh, what a sensation we caused, let me tell you! These two big guys and this little Chihuahua that, tell you the truth, I always felt favored Frank Sinatra a bit.

DINK. You know, I thought so, too. Idn't that funny?

LEO. We'd walk and we'd talk about this and that, you know, one thing or another, just to pass the time. And every once in a while we'd stop, sit on a bench.

(A beat. This is a wonderful memory.)

Take in the sun.

DINK. Walt loved to take in the sun.

LEO. Just the three of us.

(beat)

Me and Randy – we had this sorta unspoken agreement. We got along O.K., you know? I mean, we weren't best friends. More like…well, associates, really. But did that little guy love Walt! Kee-ripes…Randy loved Walt so much he'd cry – my hand to the Bible, that little dog would break down in tears of happiness just at the sight of Walt. You remember that?

PERRY. It was touching.

LEO. Old Walt'd say "Who loves you, Randy?" And Randy, you know, had those great big little Chihuahua eyes and they'd just fill up with tears of gratitude and he'd shake his tail so much his little heiney would be dancin back and forth and all the time these tears of joy just streamin down his little face. Oh – it was a sight to behold.

(a pause)

LEO. Almost 9 years they went everywhere together. The last year or so, Randy got the arthritis in his back so bad Walt had to carry him every place till finally the pain got so bad he had to…

(a pause)

When Randy died – you guys remember this?

(The guys nod.)

Had a little memorial service for him, right here. Perry said the nicest prayer, I said a few words. The least I could do – I mean, hell – the three of us had had some kinda times together, you know? And Walt…? I wanna tell you, Joel.

DINK. It was rough.

LEO. Walt was, for a period of time, kinda lost – this lost and lonely man. But finally, maybe a month after Randy checked out, outta the blue, he calls me on the horn and says to me "Leo, you gotta have something pretty terrific in the first place to feel like hell when you lose it. Randy was a pisser but it's time to move on."

DINK. Like I said, Walt had it figured out.

LEO. I'm tellin you, Joel. How many of us got the chance to be so fortunate? Randy was just this big-eyed, nervous little dog with a slick toupee and a nifty outfit but to have a companion like that? A rare and precious thing.

(NICK gets up and walks away.)

DINK. Hey, Leo.

(He motions to NICK. A pause as the guys watch NICK. Finally…)

LEO. Oh. Uh…hey, Nicky – I ran into Sara the other day.

NICK. That so?

LEO. Over at Wendys. Wednesday. No – Thursday. Thursday night I went to Wendys. They got that potato bar for God's sake. Damnedest thing – they give you this baked potato and then you pile on all the cheese and bacon and onions and sour cream and chives, Nicky, chives! I'm tellin' you it's just a potato but it's a meal in and of itself. Anyhow –

(takes a big gulp of his soda)

I'd just sat down when Sara walks in with Mikey – oh what a great youngster *he* is!

DINK. He's a pip, Nicky.

LEO. Oh, one in a million, kid. One in a million.

(He continues.)

And, after they got their food, they sit down not far from me and she asks me how I'm doin' and I say "Sara – I heard about you and Nicky and I'm heartbroken. I'm absolutely heartbroken." And she says – now listen to this, Nicky – she says "Yeah – I know. It's been hard on all of us." Meaning it was hard on her too. She said that, Nicky – and so I said to her "Nicky's havin' a terrible time, Sara. He's off the sauce and he's going to those meetings but he's feelin' pretty low." And then she says – now get this – Sara says "I'm sorry to hear that cause I don't wish him no harm." I mean, Nicky – huh? How about that?

NICK. There ain't no chance of anything happening. Trust me.

LEO. There's always a chance, kid.

NICK. Leo, she's erasing me.

DINK. Wha...she's – she's what?

NICK. I'm being erased. All the family pictures? She's taking me outta them.

LEO. What are you talking?

NICK. Like, there's a picture we took at Sears last year with me and her and Mikey only now it's just her and Mikey.

LEO. Oh, Nick.

DINK. *(softly)* Christ on a bike.

NICK. I'm pickin up Mikey for McDonalds the other day and I happen to see the picture on the mantel. And it looked different. Like something was missin. I stared at it for like 5 minutes before I realized what was missin – me. I says "What the hell?" and Sara says "Don't give me any shit, Nick. I'm gettin' it done to alla them. I'm wipin' you out."

PERRY. How can that happen?

NICK. Computer. Fucking computer at the camera shop. You bring in a picture, they push some buttons, and I fuckin disappear.

DINK. *(Nodding his head. To* **JOEL.***)* They do it in the movies all the time.

NICK. Yeah? Well, now they're doin it to me. Christ.

(**DINK** *starts to cross to* **NICK.***)*

Don't hug me, Dink.

DINK. O.K.

(a beat)

NICK. Maybe later.

DINK. Sure, Nick.

LEO. Jeez, kid, I don't know what to say.

NICK. You got no idea what it feels like to get erased. To be turned invisible. It fuckin hurts.

(an awkward pause)

LEO. Hey, hold the bus – what about Joel?

JOEL. What?

LEO. Joel could help.

NICK. Who?

PERRY. *(pointing to* **JOEL***)* Joel.

JOEL. *(realizing)* Oh no –

NICK. "Joel?" What the hell could "Joel" do?

JOEL. *(quickly)* Nothing. Nothing. There's nothing I can do.

LEO. You kidding me? Loopholes, Joel. Loopholes. Clauses. Injunctions. Writs. Precedent. Suits, Joel. Suits.

NICK. What're you talkin', Leo?

JOEL. Nick, I'm terribly sorry about your domestic situation, I truly am, but there is nothing I can do.

NICK. Fine. Who's asking? What're you talkin about, Leo?

LEO. Nicky, you probably got rights. Just because you screwed up your life don't mean you got no rights. Maybe it's against the law to erase someone without their permission.

NICK. So?

LEO. So he's a lawyer, Nick.

NICK. *What?*

LEO. One phone call from Joel would probably take care of it. I bet he's a hell of a lawyer.

(**NICK** *turns on* **JOEL** *and bellows incoherently.*)

JOEL. What? What?

PERRY. Jesus, Nick – !

NICK. You're a lawyer –

JOEL. But –

NICK. You just moved to town –

JOEL. Well –

NICK. You're that bastard Buck Drum's lawyer!

(**NICK** *bellows again.*)

DINK. Look out!

NICK. *(pointing at* **JOEL***)* He's suing me!

LEO. What?

JOEL. I didn't know!

NICK. Bloodsucker!

JOEL. *(starting for the door)* Help!

(**NICK** *cuts off* **JOEL***'s escape.*)

LEO. Nicky –

NICK. You're trying to ruin me!

JOEL. I didn't know –

NICK. The only thing I got left you're trying to take from me! A man without a job is less than ruined!

LEO. *(crossing toward* **NICK***)* Nick, you gotta watch it. Remember your probation!

JOEL. Probation?

NICK. *(to LEO)* Get back!

JOEL. What probation?

DINK. Look out Joel –

JOEL. Somebody do something!

LEO. Nick! Nick! You can't. You can't do nothin to him. You know that.

JOEL. Nick's on probation??

PERRY. Think about it, Nick. Think about it.

LEO. You can't lay a finger on him.

(Beat. Then…)

NICK. *(slowly advancing on JOEL)* I don't got to.

LEO. What're you talkin?

NICK. Relax – I'm not goin' to touch him, alright?

DINK. Nicky –

(NICK continues to slowly cross towards JOEL.)

NICK. Let me tell you something, pal –

(NICK makes a sudden movement with his hand towards JOEL – who flinches mightily, throwing up his arms as if to protect himself and shouting in surprise.)

JOEL. Augghh!

PERRY. Nick –

NICK. *(pointing his finger menacingly towards JOEL.)* You're no Walter!

JOEL. I never said I –

(NICK throws another hand towards JOEL. JOEL, still backing, flinches again, this time crashing into the table. Grabbing his back – or hip or whatever.)

Augghh!

NICK. Walter was a hell of a guy.

(Another flick and, this time, JOEL's mighty flinch causes him to pop himself in the nose with his own fist. JOEL yelps in pain.)

JOEL. *(Grabbing his nose and staggering backwards.)* My nose!
PERRY. Jesus Christ!

    *(**NICK** continues to slowly pursue **JOEL**.)*

NICK. A hell of a guy!

    *(Another quick movement and, this time, the battered **JOEL** flinches so badly he topples backwards over a chair and crashes to the floor.)*

JOEL. *(groveling, near the wall)* Please!

    *(**NICK** is now standing over **JOEL**.)*

NICK. Don't think for a moment you can walk in here, wear Walt's cap, and then expect me to forget all about Walter. Walter was a champ, pal.

LEO. Nick!

NICK. A champ!

    *(**NICK** administers a final flick, causing **JOEL** to flinch and bang his head into the wall.)*

PERRY. *(crossing to **JOEL**)* My God –

LEO. Jesus Christ, Nicky! What did you do?

NICK. Didn't lay a finger on him!

PERRY. He beat the hell outta himself!

JOEL. Am I bleeding?

DINK. Take it easy –

PERRY. Hold your head back like this you'll be fine.

JOEL. I'm bleeding. I'm bleeding!

LEO. Whadidhe? Bust his nose?

JOEL. Shit! I'm in hell!

NICK. You ain't in Hell, pal. Believe me – I been in Hell and it ain't nothin like this!

JOEL. I don't know where I am, I don't know why I'm here, I can't leave, and I just beat myself up! This is hell!

    (dabbing his nose with a tissue)

    Shit – I'm telling you, if my nose is broken –

NICK. What? You gonna sue me?

JOEL. This is assault.

NICK. You want your pound of flesh? Why don't you just take it now and get it over with?

(Rolls up his sleeve, lays his arm on the table, then grabs his hand saw.)

Huh? How about this?

PERRY. Oh, for Christ's sake –

(with a weary sigh)

Drop the saw, Nick.

NICK. Get back – I'll do it!

DINK. Nick –

NICK. I'll do it!

LEO. *(loudly)* Nick!

(Pause. Then, calmly.)

You're outta control, kid, and you gotta get a grip or else you are gonna lose everything. No screwing around – you will have nothin. At least right now, you got us but you keep this shit up? I don't know. You understand?

*(A pause. Finally, **NICK** grabs a board in both hands and slams it a couple of times on the table. He then hits it with his hammer several times.)*

JOEL. My God!

*(**NICK** now takes his handsaw and begins to saw the board until he saws through. He then picks up the scrap, walks to the window, opens it, and, after a glare at **JOEL**, tosses the scrap out. He then crosses back to the remainder of the offending board and hits the board a couple of times with his hammer. Spent, he turns toward the men, bellows one more time, then exits.)*

(A tense pause. Finally…)

DINK. Nick has a hard time expressing his anger appropriately.

JOEL. *(with stunned sarcasm)* Is it a "condition?"

DINK. *(honestly)* Yeah – I think it is.

PERRY. Let me get you another tissue.

LEO. Dink?

> (**DINK** *crosses to the window and looks out.*)

DINK. He's sitting on the curb.

LEO. Alright, boys – circumstances –

> *(gestures to the remnants of his soda)*

– hand me that, will you Perry? – circumstances are dire, extremely dire.

> (**PERRY** *hands* **LEO** *the soda.*)

DINK. It was only a matter of time.

LEO. The question is, what are we going to do? Any suggestions?

JOEL. Any suggestions? The man is certifiable and I am bleeding!

> *(sputtering)*

I mean…Jesus Christ – he's on *probation?*

LEO. D.U.I.

DINK. He had a little problem but he's dealing with it.

JOEL. That's dealing with it?

LEO. Better than it was, right Dink?

DINK. Sad but true I don't think he's ever been happier.

LEO. So what about it? Joel?

JOEL. I'm bleeding from the nostrils! I have absolutely nothing to suggest!

LEO. *(with a sigh)* Ah, Joel.

JOEL. What?

LEO. You disappoint me.

JOEL. You don't know me well enough to be disappointed!

> *(A pause. Then…)*

LEO. Perry –

PERRY. *(shaking his head)* Nope – I can't.

DINK. Just a coupla words –

PERRY. I don't do that anymore. He should see a clergyman.

LEO. What're you talking?

PERRY. I'm an insurance salesman!

LEO. I work shipping and receiving – so what? Just cause you got a trade don't mean you resign from bein' one of the guys! Perry, it's been you and Nicky, Nicky and you since you was kids, I mean come on. There have been times – listen to me, Perry – there have been times in the life of you and in the life of Nick – and you know what I'm talking about – where if it wasn't for the fact that you and Nicky were closer than brothers? Kee-ripes – neither one of you woulda made it out alive! I'm telling you – Nicky's hurtin, kid. He's hurtin bad.

PERRY. So what? Big deal! Everybody hurts, Leo! Everybody. Everybody. And they all want someone to make it better, they all want comfort, they all want reassurance but I don't do that anymore! I am a weak…weak, weak man. I am a man without…without…

(Pause as he struggles to find the right words. Then, a realization.)

I'm a man without. That's it. I am without. Empty. There is nothing left.

(Ends up mightily shaking his fist. Beat. Then…)

And Walt knew.

LEO. Wait a minute. Walt? What…?

(beat)

Perry, you got fired not long after Walter croaked. What's he got to do with it?

(pause)

PERRY. I sat there and watched Walt turn blue. I watched him die. I couldn't do anything.

LEO. Oh.

PERRY. I just sat there. I was paralyzed. The only thing I could think was "Christ – Walt fell right on top of Dink! That must hurt like hell!"

DINK. I'm alright now, Perry.

PERRY. No prayers. No words of comfort. Nothing.

LEO. Are you kidding me, kid? Kee-ripes, you did an incredibly kind act. You sat beside him, you held his hand and when Walt checked out, you were there. He musta known. You held his hand, Perry.

PERRY. He had me in a death grip, Leo! He reached out, grabbed my hand, and almost crushed it. The man did not want to go. I didn't want to hold his hand – hell, I didn't even want to touch him! I was trying to pull away but he wouldn't let go!

(pause)

PERRY. *(cont.)* My God. How lonely that must've been. The one moment in a man's life when you'd want somebody with you, I did nothing.

LEO. Perry, Walter dropped dead. Literally. Nobody knew what to do, you know? We were all running around like idiots – with the exception of Dink, of course.

DINK. I wanted to – I just couldn't get up!

LEO. Walt died of a massive coronary. No way you coulda stopped that. Nothing you coulda done.

PERRY. You know what happened? I was sitting there and it looked like Walt was trying to say something. So I put my ear next to his lips and Walt whispered "Why?" "Why?" And all I could say was "I don't know."

LEO. So maybe he meant "Why? Why did I fall on my keys?"

DINK. I did feel a poke there, Perry.

PERRY. No. The man was scared. And he died alone. He didn't want to go.

LEO. Who does? When my time comes, I'll beat the shit outta God himself if I think it'll buy me a few more minutes. Christ, Perry – you think people die like they do in the movies – all peaceful and smiling and noble and shit? Walt grabbed life with both mitts. No way Walter would go out happy.

(beat)

LEO. Whaddya say, Perry? Come on. I'm not talkin some kinda sermon. Nicky doesn't need a preacher – and he doesn't need an insurance salesman. Just…just – be a pal. That's all I'm asking. That's all.

(No answer. **LEO** *and* **DINK** *look at each other.* **DINK** *shrugs.)*

*(***NICK*** enters without a word, quickly crosses to his tool box, gets out his tape measure, and proceeds to measure a board. He does this with great concentration for a moment then…)*

NICK. You see, the thing is…the thing is my kid. He's not goin to remember.

LEO. What're you talkin? I've seen the way he looks at you. Mikey don't need a picture to remember the old man.

NICK. Yeah, that's right, Leo. He's gonna remember me like *this* or – goddamnit – like I was before. But he ain't gonna remember me like I was in that picture when I was cleaned up, when I had on that tie, and I was standing there in Sears with this proud look on my face because…because I loved my family so damned much. He won't remember that cause I won't be in the picture. I'll be erased.

(Beat – then, heartbroken.)

But the pictures in his *mind*. The pictures in his mind. They can't erase them, goddamnit.

*(***LEO*** looks to* **PERRY** *who looks away.)*

*(***JOEL*** has been watching. He wipes his nose gingerly and crosses to* **NICK** *and clears his throat.* **JOEL** *takes deep breath and speaks with growing confidence.)*

JOEL. Strictly speaking, all photographs taken during a marriage would be considered marital property owned in common by both spouses and neither can sell it, dispose of it, or alter it without the others expressed written consent. At the very least, you have a legal right to have copies of the pictures made before she alters their appearance in any way. If she persists, you could have her served with an order of cease and desist. I mean…

(beat)

Well – you wouldn't have to be…erased.

(LEO and DINK look to each other. Impressed.)

NICK. *(nodding numbly)* Oh.

(beat)

O.K.

(JOEL walks away.)

Hey…

(JOEL turns.)

Thanks.

(JOEL nods and walks away. NICK and PERRY. look at each other for a long moment as PERRY struggles mightily. Walks over to NICK. Finally…)

PERRY. Nick…I'm an insurance salesman. I…

(He is at a loss for words. Tries to speak a couple of times. Finally, he looks closely at his friend. A slight smile. A long pause. Then, with great relief…)

NICK. Shit. Thanks, Perry.

(Pause. Some kind of order now restored, LEO crosses back to his chair and DINK returns to his solitaire. JOEL takes off Walt's cap, gets his briefcase and coat, and crosses to LEO. He stands for an awkward moment before leo. Finally, JOEL crosses over to LEO.)

JOEL. Leo…

LEO. *(very impressed)* Boy, that was terrific there.

(JOEL shrugs slightly.)

Sorry it didn't work out, kid. Thanks for dropping by, though.

(JOEL turns to go, stops, then comes back to LEO.)

JOEL. Before I go –

(mystified fumbling)

Why? I mean…why?

(A pause. Then…)

LEO. You watch much TV, Joel?

JOEL. Wh…what?

LEO. Television. Do you watch it?

JOEL. Yes. Yes, I watch television. Yes.

LEO. I'm a fan of those nature programs. Saw this animal show on TV coupla weeks ago. Maybe you guys caught it. You know – the one they got on channel 4 Sunday afternoons with that guy? You know – the one used to be on that cop show?

DINK. The one about the two cops?

LEO. *(simultaneously)* – the two cops. Sure.

PERRY. *(recognition)* Ohhh. Right.

NICK. That was a great show.

LEO. Terrific show. Anyhow, this guy's got this animal show now and what he does, see, is he goes on these trips to Africa and Australia and – I don't know – Korea, maybe, places like that. And he takes a camera crew and a celebrity co-host and they film the animals of the wild and talk about the celebrity co-host's latest movie. A fascinating program.

DINK. It's a good show, Leo.

LEO. You seen it then.

DINK. Yeah – it's a good show.

LEO. You see the one on elephants? Oh boy, let me tell you.

NICK. I like elephants.

LEO. Remarkable creatures, Joel – very large, very mysterious. Elephants have been around for many, many years and there's still much we don't understand about them.

JOEL. Is that so?

LEO. Absolutely. For example –

(He suddenly pauses, throws up one hand to signal that they should wait.)

DINK. Leo?

*(**LEO** holds up his hand a bit longer then, finally, belches loudly.)*

JOEL. God.

(**LEO** *continues.*)

LEO. For example, on this show they said that elephants make these mysterious sighs.

JOEL. Sighs?

LEO. Well...moans. Sighing moans.

JOEL. I didn't know that.

LEO. Oh sure. But the thing is, to the human ear? They're invisible.

JOEL. What's invisible?

LEO. The sighs.

JOEL. Invisible? Invisible sighs?

LEO. Yeah. You can't hear them. You could be standing right next to an elephant and he could be sighing these sighs and moaning these moans and you wouldn't know it. You would be unaware.

JOEL. How about that.

LEO. But to another elephant? These sighs are music. Sad, sad music comin' in loud and clear over hundreds and hundreds of miles.

JOEL. Hundreds of miles?

LEO. How about that, huh? See, elephants do this, see, they do all this moaning and sighing when they're lonely, when they feel their heart breaking, when they feel like they can't go on for even another minute.

NICK. How they know this?

LEO. Scientists.

NICK. Oh. Right.

LEO. These invisible, incredibly sad sighs float out over mountains and plains far and wide, until, finally, they connect with other elephants. And here's the remarkable thing. When they hear this, they drop whatever they're doing and come together to offer comfort. They come together.

NICK. Get outta town.

LEO. Scientists tell us this. That's what they said on the program.

PERRY. Incredible.

LEO. Let me tell you what…that is a noble thing.

NICK. Elephants.

PERRY. Magnificent creatures.

DINK. You ever see that cartoon about that flying elephant named Dumbo? It was called DUMBO, I think.

LEO. So…you see what I'm saying, Joel?

*(a stunned beat as **JOEL** realizes)*

JOEL. Oh, come off it!

LEO. Hey, Joel, fact of the matter is you don't know why you're here because I never asked you to come.

*(**JOEL** looks at him, disbelieving.)*

Hand to the Bible. I told you about Walt, I told you about the guys, I got a feeling you wanted to drop by but I didn't ask you to. Think about it – you know it's true, Joel.

JOEL. No. No, no, Leo. No. You said…I mean, you…

LEO. None of us know. No one plans it. We just get together when we feel the need.

JOEL. That is patently preposterous.

LEO. Dink –

DINK. *(looking up from his game)* Hmmm?

LEO. Why are you here?

DINK. Couldn't tell you, Leo. Just woke up this A.M. and knew what I had to do.

LEO. Nicky?

NICK. *(with a shrug)* Where else would I go?

LEO. What about you, Perry?

PERRY. I quit questioning it a long time ago.

LEO. What else are we going to do? We need all the help we can get. I mean, look at us –

(with a laugh)

We're a pretty pathetic group of men!

JOEL. Then what am *I* doing here?

(The guys just shrug.)

Right. That's what I thought.

(picks up his briefcase, gets his coat)

Thank you for the…invitation to join you but…

(a beat)

I'm a very private person. I don't…well.

(Turns to go. A beat, then, to **NICK**…*)*

JOEL. *(cont.)* If the pictures are community property you have a legal right to at least have copies of the pictures made before she alters their appearance in any way. I believe that could be easily contested.

NICK. Yeah, O.K. Thanks.

*(***JOEL*** turns and, resigned and without rancor…)*

See you in court.

(A beat. **JOEL** *heads for the door and stops. Another beat. Finally, having reached a decision,* **JOEL** *crosses back to the others.)*

JOEL. *(a quiet announcement)* They used to push me down.

LEO. Beg pardon, Joel?

JOEL. *(quietly)* When I was a little boy. They used to push me down. The other children, on the playground. During recess. You see, I had a stutter and the children used to make fun of the way I…the way I talked. They called me "Ja-ja-joel." And then they'd chase me. All over the playground. My whole class, maybe 25 boys and girls. A whole herd of kids. I'd run and run but sooner or later they'd catch me and push me down.

(beat)

And then jump on top of me. In a big pile. I was at the bottom. *(beat)* It was hard to breathe sometimes.

LEO. Kee-ripes, that must've been terrible, Joel.

DINK. Kids. What can you do?

PERRY. They can be very cruel.

JOEL. Ever since, whenever I feel threatened I...well, that's why I...flinch...so big. You understand.

NICK. Oh sure.

JOEL. Self-protection.

(beat)

I just thought you should know that.

*(Unsure of what to do next, **JOEL** stands for a moment, then turns and exits.)*

*(A long pause, then an agitated **JOEL** returns. The guys watch him as he struggles. Finally...)*

JOEL. I can't leave! I'm absolutely incapable of leaving! This place is a vortex of lethargy!

DINK. I know. Isn't it nice?

*(**JOEL** sits – a man with much on his mind. A long pause. Finally, to no one in particular...)*

JOEL. Every morning, I wake up and for a few moments I feel somehow...disoriented. I lie in bed, eyes closed, and I'm a blank. I forget where I am. Nothing hurts. I feel...nothing. I remember nothing.

PERRY. *(with a sympathetic nod)* Yeah.

JOEL. And that is the only time of the day I am not afraid. I look foward to those few moments. But as soon as I realize I'm not afraid I remember who I am and what I am...and I realize that I'm petrified and I remember that I am always petrified.

NICK. Tell me about it.

*(**DINK** walks over to **JOEL** and pats him on the back.)*

JOEL. I woke up this morning, looked at my wife, looked out my window at my backyard...and said to myself "What the hell am I doing? I can't do this anymore. I have to leave." And I started...well – musing about how easy it would be to just walk out the front door, drive to the bank, take out all our savings, gas up the car and just...hit the road. Nothing was stopping me.

LEO. *(sympathetically)* Kee-ripes.

JOEL. It was so compelling. Just the idea of leaving everything behind, starting all over again somewhere else.

DINK. *(sympathetically)* Christ on a bike, I hate having thoughts like that.

JOEL. I even chose an alias! "Logan Douglas." I mean, Logan Douglas? That frightened me more than anything. Why would I come up with an alias unless I was serious?

PERRY. My alias is Earl Perkins.

DINK. I go by Harry Belafonte.

(an explanation)

Milly loves calypso music.

JOEL. I love my wife. I love my family. The last thing in the world I want to do is leave. My God. But –

(A pause. Then...)

What am I doing? What the hell am I doing?

NICK. Just try to hold on to the magic, pal.

PERRY. Yeah. Give it some time. You'll be alright.

DINK. Just let me know if there's anything I can do.

LEO. You're among friends here, Joel. You're among friends.

*(A pause as **JOEL** looks around the room. **PERRY** is reading one of his books, **NICK** is measuring a board, **DINK** is happily playing solitaire, and **LEO** is munching his taco.)*

*(**JOEL** looks down and sees Walt's red "soft cap." He picks it up, looks at it, then puts it on. He sits silently, contentedly lost.)*

End of Play

COSTUME PLOT

Joel
Dark suit
White shirt
Conservative tie
Wing-tip shoes
Overcoat
"Walt's Hat: - red Army "soft cap" with "Walt" stitched on the side, festooned with ribbons and buttons

Dink
Corduroy pants
Cardigan sweater
Plaid work shirt
Horn-rimmed glasses

Perry
Hooded gray sweatshirt
Dark windbreaker
Khaki slacks
Jogging shoes

Nick
Baseball cap
Pittsburgh Steelers jacket
Work shirt
Long underwear shirt
Blue jeans
Work boots

Leo
"Elmer Fudd" hunting cap
Insulated overcoat
Flannel shirt
Corduroy pants
"Comfortable" shoes

PERSONAL PROPS:

Dink
- Wrench
- Deck of playing cards
- Wallet
- Photo of "Milly"

Joel
- Handkerchief
- Briefcase
- Styrofoam coffee cup
- Stack of paperback books
- Business card
- Tissue

Nick
- Toolbox
- Short 2x4's
- Tape measure
- Hammer
- Nails
- Work apron
- Hand saw

Leo
- Taco Bell bag
- Paper Taco Bell cup with soda
- Taco Bell nachos
- Container of melted cheese

SET PROPS

Radiator
Assortment of folding chairs
Wooden "card" table
Stuffed chair
Construction debris
Saw horse
A-frame ladder
Flag stand
Assortment of boxes
Large trash can with boards and construction debris
Paint cans

Off-stage
American flag on pole
Steamer trunk
Canned sodas
Coffee in coffee cups

**Also by
Ed Simpson...**

Additional Particulars

The Battle of Shallowford

The Comet of St. Loomis

A Point of Order

Please visit our website **samuelfrench.com** for complete
descriptions and licensing information